STARRING

HARVEST
WANNADOGOOD
THE FARMER

Harvest the farmer provided fresh fruits and vegetables for all of Midlandia. Farming gave Harvest's body lots of exercise. "But I also like to exercise my mind!" he always said.

That is why Harvest loved
Vincent's art shows. Vincent
was a wonderful artist. Harvest
enjoyed looking at his work and
thinking about it.

"**Wow!**" said Harvest as
he reached the gallery. "It looks
like the whole town showed up!"

Vincent led Harvest and the other guests on a tour of the gallery. "This is amazing!" thought Harvest. "I like each piece of art better than the last."

After some time, Vincent stopped the tour. "We will
take a short break now to enjoy some cookies and music," he
announced. "Afterward, I will take everyone around the corner
to the back of the gallery. There, I will unveil my masterpiece!"
That sounded very exciting to Harvest! He did
not think he could wait.

"What's the harm in sneaking a little peek?" wondered Harvest as he tiptoed away from the crowd.

"Where are you off to?"
Vincent called after him. He'd been spotted!

"Umm..." stammered Harvest. "I'm just going to wash my hands."

"Very well," replied Vincent. "You should always wash up before you eat."

Harvest could not believe what he had done! He had never told a fib before. "But it is only because I like Vincent's art so much," he assured himself.

"Vincent's masterpiece is
right back here..." thought Harvest.
Watching the crowd, he tiptoed
backward around the corner.

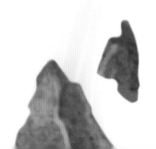

Crash! "Oh, no!" cried Harvest. He had
bumped into a sculpture and knocked it to the floor.
"I've ruined Vincent's masterpiece!"

No one out front had heard the crash. "But they'll find out soon enough," sighed Harvest. "I wasn't even supposed to be back here. How can I face Vincent now?"

"You don't have to," said a voice. Harvest turned in surprise. It was one of those sneaky Inks! "You don't have to tell Vincent," said the Ink.

"What do you mean?" asked Harvest.

"Just say that you had nothing to do with breaking this sculpture," the Ink suggested. "That way, Vincent will not get angry with you."

"I already fibbed once tonight." said Harvest. "I won't fib again."

"If you tell Vincent the truth, he'll be very upset," said the Ink.

"He might not want to be your friend anymore."

"I am worried about that," admitted Harvest.

"You should blame someone else!" declared the Ink.

"I can't get an innocent Midlandian in **trouble**," said Harvest.

"Then here's what you can tell him!" the Ink exclaimed. "Tell Vincent that you heard a strange noise, so you came to check it out. When you turned the corner, you saw a wild monkey leaping about!"

"He was hungry for bananas, so he climbed the sculpture to look for some. But there were no bananas, so the monkey got angry. You tried to stop that crazy monkey, but it smashed Vincent's masterpiece into masterpieces."

Harvest was not convinced.
"That does not seem like a good idea,"
he said. **"Telling the truth** is
just the right thing to do."
"If you don't want my advice,
then don't ask for it," sniffed the Ink.

"But I didn't ask for your advice!" said Harvest. "What are you doing here, anyway?"

The Ink's eyes went wide. "Umm..." he said, looking quite devious, "I'm here because **I love art.**"

Just then, Harvest noticed a second Ink by the wall.
"Your friend is trying to rip that painting down!" said Harvest.

"**He is not!**" insisted the Ink. "He just likes the painting so much that he is giving it a hug."

Harvest spotted a third Ink! "That one's putting Ink prints all over Vincent's work!" cried Harvest.

"**He's an art critic.**"

The music out front stopped. **"Inks! Inks!"** someone cried.

"We're spotted!" said the Inks. They dashed away just as Vincent and the others hurried in.

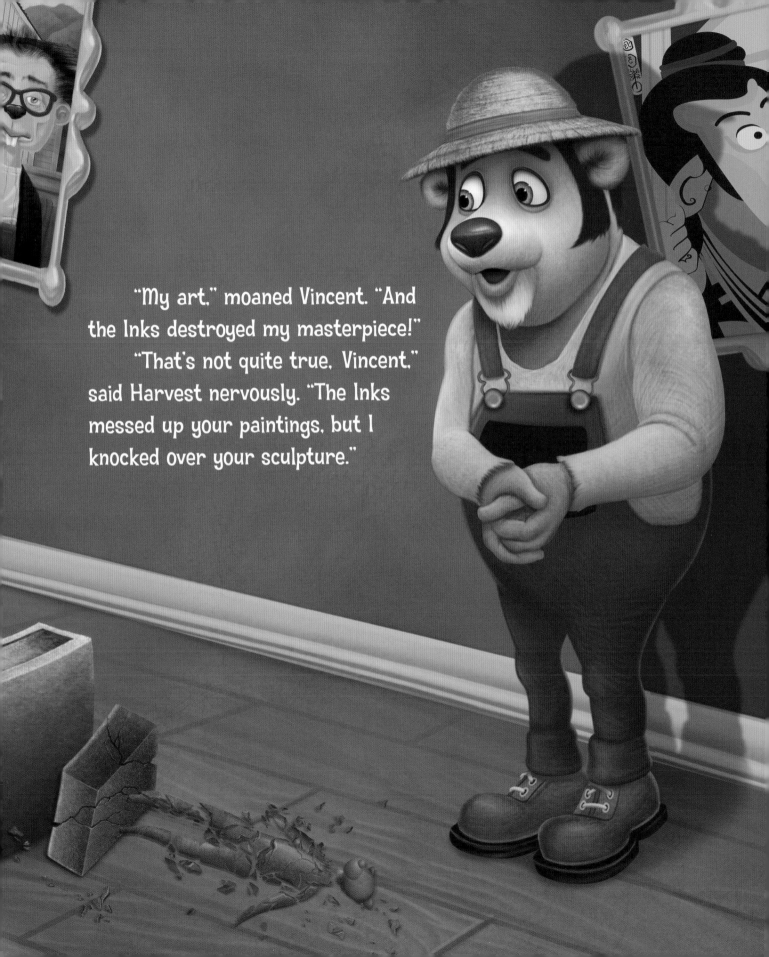

"My art," moaned Vincent. "And the Inks destroyed my masterpiece!"

"That's not quite true, Vincent," said Harvest nervously. "The Inks messed up your paintings, but I knocked over your sculpture."

Everyone was shocked!
"You did it?" asked Vincent.
"When I said I was going
to wash my hands before, I
told you a lie," said Harvest.
"I was really sneaking off to
look at your masterpiece. But
I bumped it by accident, and
it tipped over and broke.
I am so sorry."

Vincent did not know what to think. **"This show is over!"** he shouted. "Everyone go home."

The guests all filed out, but Harvest stayed behind. "It's okay if you are angry with me, Vincent," he said. "But I will do anything to make it up to you. I just have to figure out how."

Vincent watched Harvest think. Then, Vincent had a flash of inspiration. "Don't move a muscle!" he said.

Every day after working on the farm, Harvest came and sat as Vincent carved a new sculpture.

"Just sit like this?" asked Harvest.

"Just sit and think!" answered Vincent.

After some weeks, Vincent was finished.

"This sculpture looks just like me!" cried Harvest.

"I call this piece *The Friend*," said Vincent.

"I don't understand," replied Harvest.

"I was mad when you broke my first sculpture, but you acted bravely by being honest about it," said Vincent. "You could have blamed the Inks, but you took responsibility."

"All I did was tell the truth," said Harvest.

Vincent replied, "That is what a true friend always does."

Discussion Questions

Has anyone ever told a fib to you?
How did it make you feel?

What can happen when you do not tell the truth?